Winter's Eve

Love and Lights

Positive Spin Press
Rhode Island, U.S.A.

For You!
and for everyone else, too
in all of our wonderful differentness
(a potluck's no fun if everyone brings the same dish!)

For more information on each of these holidays and more
please visit
www.pappyholidays.com

Published by Positive Spin Press   Distributed by Independent Publishers Group
www.positivespinpress.com   www.ipgbook.com   1-800-888-4741

Printed in China

When winter comes

There's not much sun
So we find clever ways

To celebrate our light and love
We call them "holidays"

Eve loves All Hallows every day
                    But in the winter most
When things slow down and she has time
                    For hot cocoa and toast

But not all fairies feel that way
                    And many take vacations
They go to visit favorite spots
                    And sometimes other nations

When Eve's friends went on holiday
                    She missed them very much
But she was glad because they said
                    They'd surely keep in touch

"Delivery! From India!
　　　　From Pari's winter trip!"
Eve was so delighted
　　　　That she almost did a flip!

"Dear Eve, Wish you could be here
　　　　It's the most enchanting mood
We've helped clean up all the houses
　　　　And prepared all kinds of food!

We are lighting lamps called diyas
　　　　To provide a welcome glow
For our gods and for good fortune
　　　　It's Diwali! Don't you know?

Our noble god, blue as the sky and equally as pure
Saved our lovely goddess when a demon kidnapped her

After fourteen years away it was a joyous celebration
When this holy prince returned and finally had his coronation

Our Festival of Lights reminds us of their great return
And that light will conquer darkness is the lesson that we learn

We offer prayers, eat sweets and visit loved ones all week through
So I hope you like this nut and my Diwali lamp for you!"

One clear bright morning afterward
        A cricket rang Eve's bell
He had a singing telegram
        From Jack in Israel

"Jack is with his family
        and he wanted to send word
Of the story about Hanukkah
        in case you haven't heard!"

He hummed a bar and cleared his throat
        and sang in Cricket-ese
"Jack's sending you a message
        all about the Maccabees!

The Maccabees fought for Jews' rights to worship and to pray
When our people were oppressed and soldiers scared us every day!

Although the odds were surely stacked against the Maccabees:
A miracle! They won and brought those soldiers to their knees!

When the Jews reclaimed the temple, it was in such disrepair!
And they only had one jug of sacred oil waiting there!

One day of oil was all there was - and certainly not two
And, Oh! Another miracle! It lasted eight nights through!

Each night on our menorahs
                    We light one candle more
And play a game called dreidel
                    Which you may have seen before!"

The cricket lifted up his wings
                    And there, to Eve's delight:
Two gifts for her that Jack had sent
                    To use that very night!

She thanked the bug and ran inside
                    To eagerly show Pappy
Who was sweeping up some fairy dust
                    To make her mother happy

"Now that I've tidied up the place
Let's make up a display!
We can add these things Aunt Inga sent
Used on St. Lucia's Day

The legend says St. Lucia came
To usher in the light
For, in Sweden, where Aunt Inga lives
The winter has long nights!

With a sash across your dress
And this lit crown upon your head
You would carry buns and coffee
To your parents, in our bed!

All around the world the celebrations have begun
To remind us of the light we get to share with everyone!

This *Advent wreath* counts down the weeks with joy and expectation
To Christmas morn, when Christ was born, and yearly jubilation

This baby in a manger brought to the world much light
And grew to show, with faith in God, a blind man could have sight

$\mathcal{A}$t Christmastime in Mexico
Los Posadas will begin
When the whole town reenacts
Christ's parents' bad luck at the inns!

But, Oh! After so many tries
At last they find a place!
The farolitos light the way
As symbols of God's grace"

Pappy spoke of holidays
                   and Eve listened for hours
Then she heard a bellflower chime
                   and sniffed the smell of flowers

A flower call! For Eve! What fun!
                   Whomever could it be?
"It's Rory, Eve, and how are you?
                   I'm with my family!

We're celebrating Kwanzaa
                   And I've got so much to share
I made a special gift for you
                   With extra special care!

African-Americans all the country wide
Celebrate our heritage with reverence and with pride

In Africa, the harvest comes about this time of year
So we honor our connection and the things that we hold dear

Each light on the kinara is lit to represent
Community and family and how our effort's spent

My grandparents tell stories, we make gifts and dance and sing
As Kwanzaa's light reminds us of the strength our values bring!"

$\mathcal{N}$ow, one thing that doesn't happen
              In the wintertime, is dew
So when Eve saw one big drop
              Outside her door, well, she just knew!

"An *Asian looking drop* from Ming-Ming!
              Just watch the edges glisten!"
And she delicately picked it up
              So she could look and listen

"We're starting out our New Year right – with friends and family
With special foods and happy moods, as clean as we can be!

We venerate our ancestors and welcome good luck in
With wishes for prosperity let the New Year begin!

The new moon brings a whole new year, we've all helped set the stage
We celebrate as we all now increase one year in age!

Fireworks and firecrackers! Look – a dragon dance!
With all these lights and lamps and sounds, bad luck won't stand a chance!"

"Look at all these lights,"
          dear Pappy whispered with a grin
"Know that each one represents a light
          that's always just within

The wintertime is special
          because as our wings slow down
It reminds us every year
          to stop and take a look around

We see the brightness in the past
          each in his own tradition
That serves to find the light in you!
          That's every person's mission!"

Pappy finished, "See how much
          Each flicker adds into the light?
For, without each one – remember
          The world wouldn't be as bright!"

Eve reveled in the fact that she
          Had learned so many ways
To help share her love and light and joy with

Pappy Holidays!